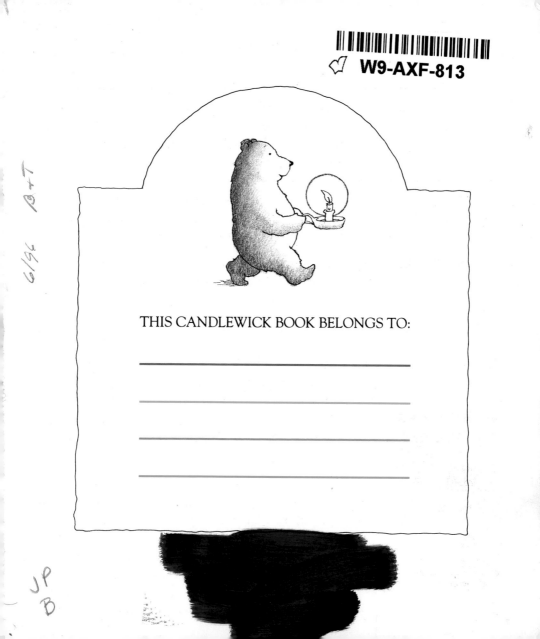

THIS CANDLEWICK BOOK BELONGS TO:

The Dog

John Burningham

CANDLEWICK PRESS

CAMBRIDGE, MASSACHUSETTS

One day a dog
we know was
left at our house
for a visit.

Mommy said
I could take
care of him.

He ate the
cat's lunch.

He licked me.

He ran into
the yard with
Daddy's shoe.

And he peed
on the flowers.

Then he
dug a hole
in the yard.

So I put him
on his leash.

I wish the
dog could
stay with me.

First U.S. paperback edition 1995

Library of Congress Cataloging-in-Publication Data

Burningham, John.
The dog / John Burningham.— 2nd U.S. ed.
Summary: A small boy enjoys looking after a dog
that is staying at his home awhile.
ISBN 1-56402-326-5(hardcover)—ISBN 1-56402-435-0(paperback)
[1. Dogs—Fiction.] I. Title.
PZ7.B936Do   1994
[E]—dc20   93-10344

2 4 6 8 10 9 7 5 3 1

Printed in Hong Kong

The pictures in this book were done in pastels, crayon, and ink.

Candlewick Press
2067 Massachusetts Avenue
Cambridge, Massachusetts 02140